by

JIM EVERHART

Photographs by Bert Brandt

CLIFFS NOTES, INC. • LINCOLN, NEBRASKA

In life there are only two good ages:
older and younger;
But at forty you're not sure which
is the better.

Jim Everhart

ISBN 0-8220-1468-8

40 is . . . that time in life when you wake up one morning, look in the bathroom mirror and suddenly realize you may *not* be prematurely gray.

40 is . . . opening a door and
going through it ahead of your
wife.

40 is . . . reading the company pension plan memos now instead of throwing them away.

40 is . . . believing it is all
right for other women to wear a
Bikini, but not your wife or
daughter.

40 is . . . talking yourself into believing your stomachache is probably something much more serious.

40 is . . . bawling out your son for getting away with the very thing you got caught at as a kid.

40 is . . . finding out you need
a partial plate and not just
three fillings.

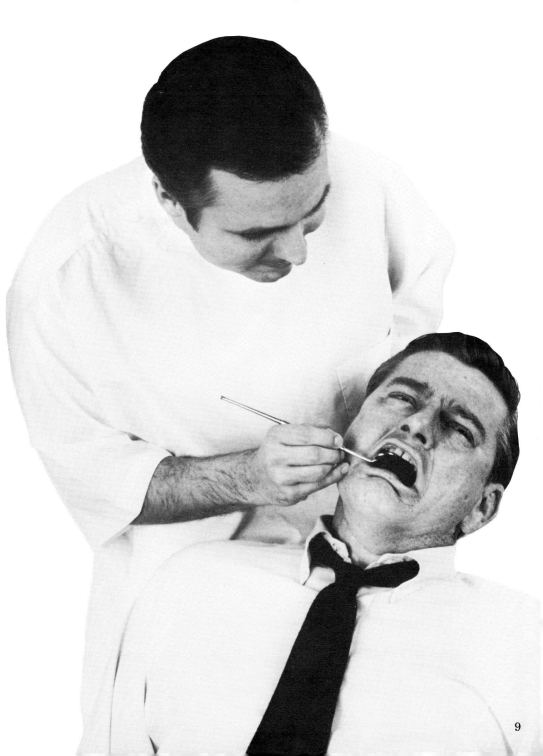

40 is . . . remembering how great your favorite motion picture was until you see it again on television.

40 is . . . receiving a Christmas card every year from somebody named "Jack" in Kansas City.

40 is . . . accepting the fact
that pants with a larger waist
size may feel more comfortable.

40 is . . . the jolt of realizing after all these years that *you* are the one who snores.

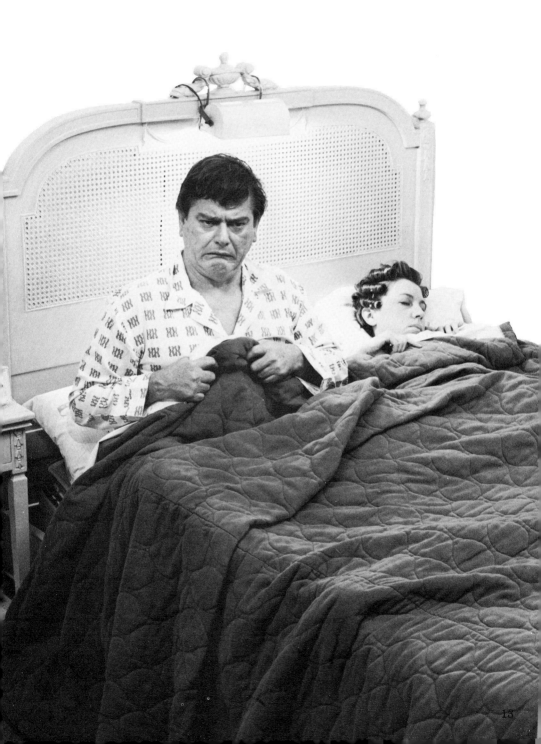

40 is . . . being completely baffled by the New Math . . . and the books that explain it.

40 is . . . reaching the conclusion that high school girls today are a lot more well-developed than when you were in school.

40 is . . . feeling a draft around your ankles.

40 is . . . overhearing your wife give as her birthdate a year so recent as to mathematically make her only 12 years old when she married you.

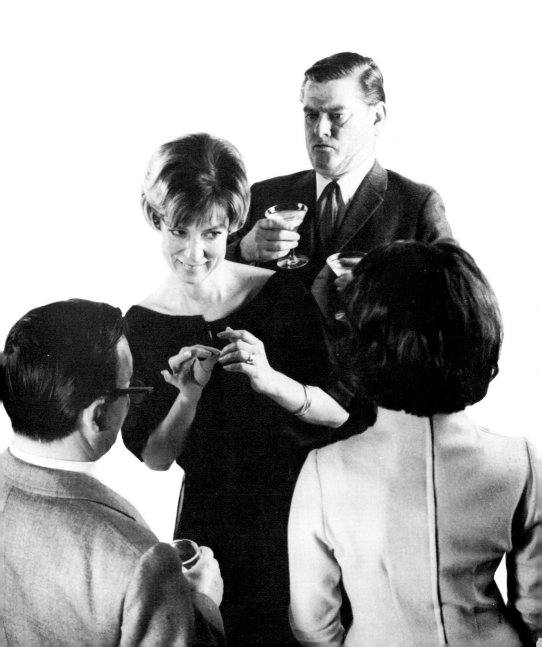

40 is . . . having everybody call you Dad except the members of your immediate family.

40 is . . . seriously thinking about giving up tennis and taking up bowling.

40 is . . . looking at a new car in the afternoon and then finding out in the evening that your daughter needs $2,000 worth of orthodontic work.

40 is . . . taking a little nap before going to bed at night.

40 is . . . the wisdom of knowing
there is nothing you can do that
is any good when your wife starts
crying.

40 is . . . going around the house turning out lights.

40 is . . . your 14-year-old son asking you why a Coke before dinner will ruin his appetite, while a martini will whet yours.

40 is . . . spending Sunday afternoon watching a pro football doubleheader and occasionally remarking to your wife what a beautiful day it is outside.

40 is . . . discovering that your arms aren't long enough for you to read a newspaper without glasses.

40 is . . . your daughter asking you what you used to look at when you listened to the radio in the days before television.

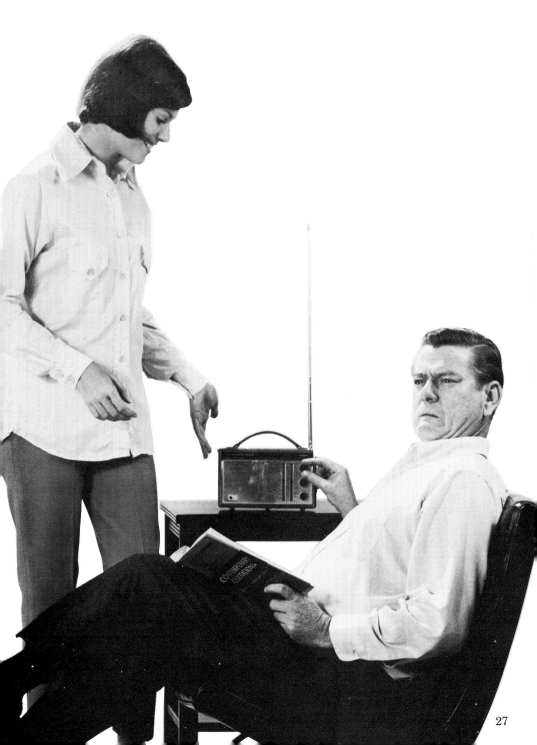

40 is . . . having that cute teenager down the street ask you and your wife to a dance . . . as chaperones.

40 is . . . adjusting to the fact that your powers of recovery after a night of drinking are not what they used to be.

40 is . . . wishing the young man your daughter
has a date with was more like you when you
were his age . . .

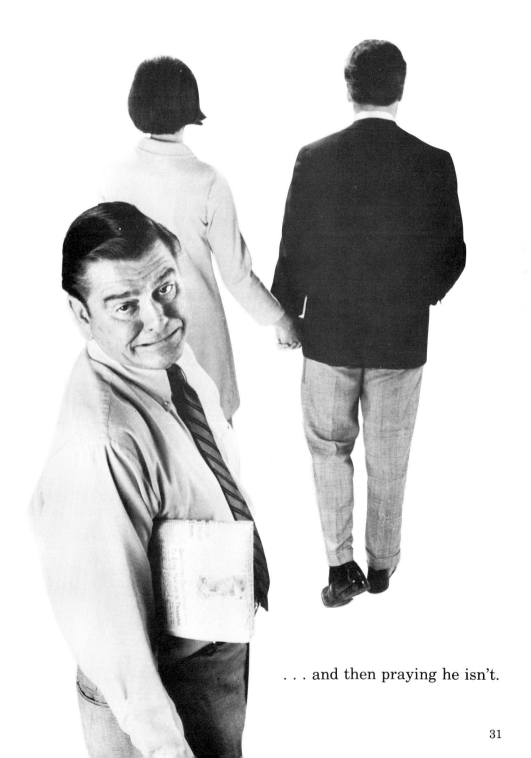

. . . and then praying he isn't.

40 is . . . giving your wife a "surely-you-don't-mean-it" look when she suggests walking five blocks to your neighbors instead of driving.

40 is . . . discussing the present world situation with a younger man and then having to identify which war you were in.

40 is . . . acknowledging the true state of affairs:
that two weeks of good, hard exercising
is *not* going to get you back in shape.

40 is . . . reading the newspaper and then saying, "I don't know what's wrong with the kids today; we never did anything like that!"

40 is . . . having your own secret recipe for making a really dry martini.

40 is . . . not recognizing anybody
at Homecoming and vice versa.

40 is . . . not knowing a single song
in the Top Forty Tunes today.

40 is . . . playing catch with your son and then not being able to raise your arm above your waist for a week.

40 is . . . knowing precisely at what point in your story your wife is going to stop believing you, fold her arms, cock her head to one side, and start tapping her foot.

40 is . . . finding more hair in your comb in the morning.

40 is . . . getting all red in the face and out of breath when you bend over to tie your shoes.

40 is . . . hearing the doctor say, "Hmmmmmm," while he has the stethoscope on your chest.

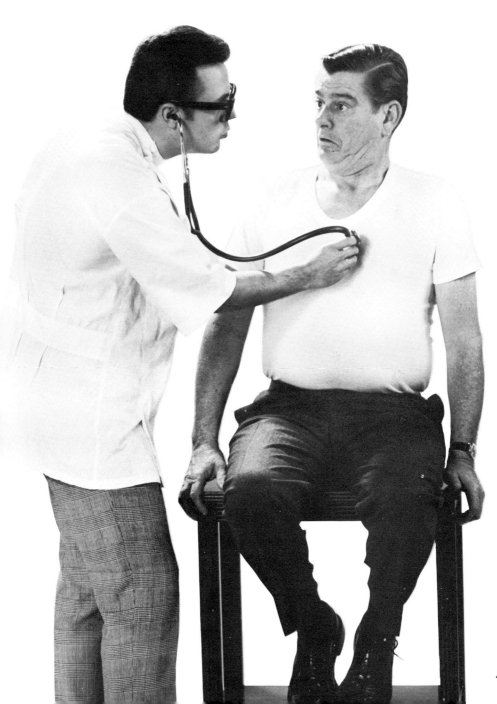

40 is . . . momentarily forgetting your wife's first name while introducing her to an absolutely gorgeous doll.

40 is . . . carrying $50 deductible car insurance for twenty years and never once having a damage claim for more than $53.10.

40 is . . . waking up during the night for various reasons instead of sleeping straight through.

40 is . . . balancing yourself in a certain way on the bathroom scales so as to get the lowest possible reading.

40 is . . . finishing this book
and knowing some of it hit home.